This item must be returned or renewed on or before the latest date shown

KT-147-983

0 028 723 07X

For James Gilbert,
who lost a tooth at Christmas. P.B.

For Codie & Kyle. G.P.

First published in 2014 by Hodder Children's Books

Text copyright © Peter Bently 2014
Illustration copyright © Garry Parsons 2014

Hodder Children's Books, 338 Euston Road, London NW1 3BH

Hodder Children's Books Australia, Level 17/207 Kent Street, Sydney, NSW 2000

The right of Peter Bently to be identified as the author and Garry Parsons as the
illustrator of this Work has been asserted by them in accordance with the Copyright,
Designs and Patents Act 1988.

All rights reserved
A catalogue record of this book is available from the British Library.

ISBN: 978 1 444 91834 2
10 9 8 7 6 5 4 3 2 1

Printed in China

Hodder Children's Books is a division of Hachette Children's Books.
An Hachette UK Company

www.hachette.co.uk

SEFTON LIBRARY
SERVICES
WITHDRAWN
002872307
1442178/00   10/10/2014
FROM STOCK
JF   £11.99
C

THE TOOTH FAIRY'S CHRISTMAS

PETER BENTLY   GARRY PARSONS

Hodder
Children's
Books

A division of Hachette Children's Books

On a cold Christmas Eve it was snowing outside
when the Tooth Fairy opened a letter and sighed.

'I was hoping to have a night in, that's the truth,
but Little Tim Tucker has just lost a tooth.'

The winter wind blasted her

this way

and that.

It blew up her knickers

and blew off her hat.

She shivered with cold from her ears to her toes, and an icicle grew on the end of her nose.

'Oh dear,' sighed the fairy. 'I seem to be lost!'
she said as she brushed off the snow and the frost.

'But hold on, what's that? Something's heading this way.
It's something that jingles. It looks like –

'Good evening!' beamed Santa. 'You do look a sight!
Why are you out on this freezing cold night?'

'I'm off to Tim Tucker's to give him a gift,
but I'm lost!'

Santa chuckled, 'I'll give you a lift!'

They came to Tim's house – but the chimney was blocked.
'Oh no,' Santa said, 'and the doors are all locked!'

'Don't worry,' the Tooth Fairy chuckled with glee,
'there's a hole in that window. Just leave it to me!'

She waggled her wand and said, 'HUBBLE-DI-FUBBLE!'

And at once they were wrapped in a shimmering bubble,

which instantly shrank to the size of a fly, and flew through the window as easy as pie.

They sailed through the house up to Tim Tucker's door,

and **POP!** they were both the same size as before.

As they entered the darkness of Tim Tucker's room
the fairy helped Santa to see in the gloom.

She whispered, 'Watch out for that train by the bed' –
but he trod on a small squeaky teddy instead!

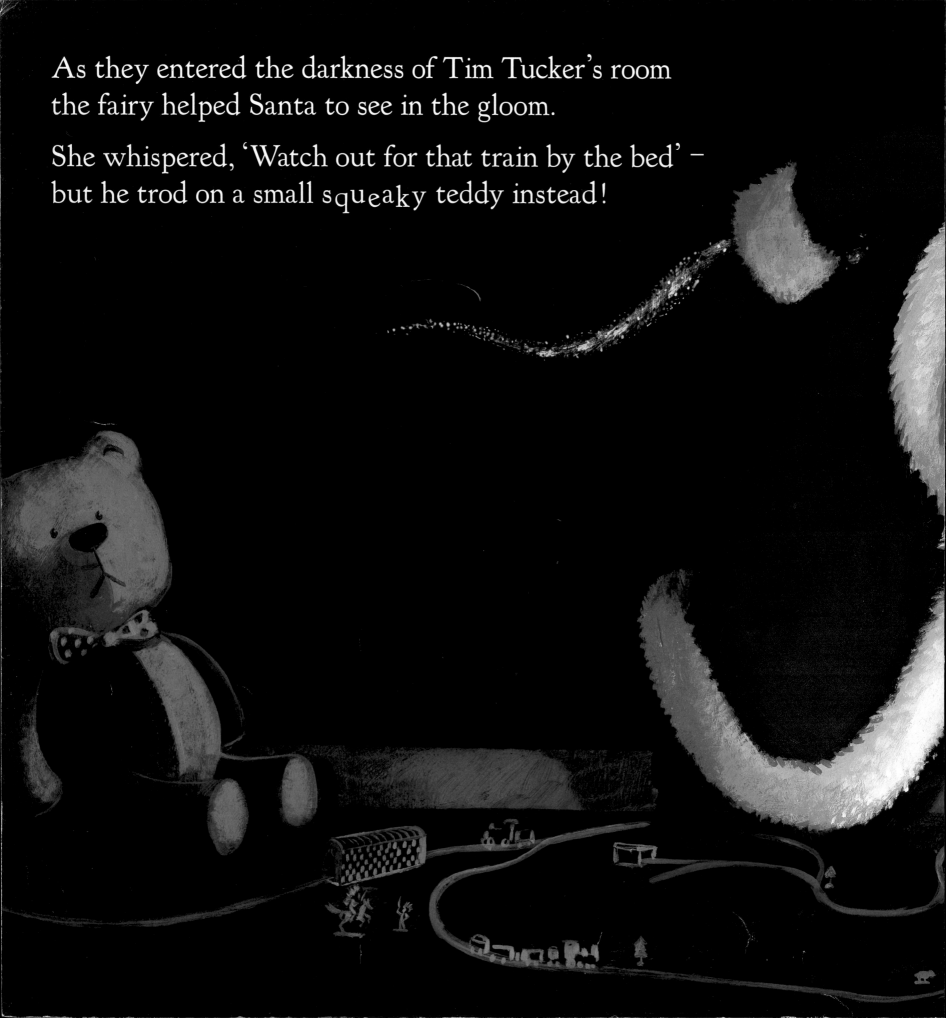

The Tooth Fairy thought,
'Don't wake up, little fellow!'
as she silently flew down to
little Tim's pillow.

She swapped the old tooth for a coin from her sack

and whispered to Santa, 'Now time to head back'.

They slipped from the bedroom but there, in the dark,
sat Tim Tucker's puppy – who started to bark!

'Yikes!' cried the Tooth Fairy. 'Now we're in trouble!
Run for it, Santa! No time for the bubble!'

They ran to the window, then what rotten luck –
as Santa climbed out his big bottom got stuck!
The Tooth Fairy pushed with a

'Heave!'

and a

'Ho!'

And together they fell in a heap in the snow.

'Giddy up, Rudolph! No time to delay!'
cried Santa as both of them leapt on the sleigh.

And off soared the sleigh through the snowstorm
once more,

till it came to a halt by the
Tooth Fairy's door.

'Thank you for helping me out in this weather,'
she said. 'It was lots of fun working together!'

'And thank you,' said Santa, 'for helping me, too.
I couldn't have left Tim his gift without you.'

'Night-night then, dear Santa,' the Tooth Fairy said,
and soon she was fast asleep, tucked up in bed.
So she didn't hear someone slip in, in his socks...

and reach in his sack for a brightly-wrapped box,
and lay it down silently under her tree.

'Sleep tight,' said Santa. 'Merry Christmas from me!'